The Birth of Nanabosho

The Birth of Nanabosho

Joseph McLellan

illustrated by Jim Kirby

PEMMICAN
PUBLICATIONS
INC.

Pemmican Publications gratefully acknowledges the assistance accorded to its publishing program by the Manitoba Arts Council, the Province of Manitoba – Department of Culture, Heritage and Tourism, Canada Council for the Arts and Canadian Heritage – Book Publishing Industry Development Program.

Printed and Bound in Canada.
First Printing: 1989   Second Printing: 1991   Third Printing: 2009   Fourth Printing: 2015

Library and Archives Canada Cataloguing in Publication

McLellan, Joseph

   The Birth of Nanabosho

   (The Nanabosho series : aniko tipachimowin; 1)
   ISBN: 978-0-921827-00-9

1. Nanabozho (Legendary character) – Legends. 2.
Ojibwa Indians – Legends★. I. Kirby, Jim, ill. II.
Title. III Series

PS8575.L44B5 1988   j398.2'1   C89-098014-4
PZ8.1.M354Bi 1988

PEMMICAN PUBLICATIONS INC.
Committed to the promotion of Metis culture and heritage

150 Henry Avenue, Winnipeg, Manitoba R3B 0J7, Canada
www.pemmican.mb.ca

Ni widagaymaagaan
Onje
Matrine
Jigwa
Dianna
nidaanis
Kikina kaie
Anishinabe abinochiiak
Owa keenawa onje
masenaagaan.

This book is for
my wife Matrine,
my daughter Dianna,
and all Ojibway children
everywhere.

It began to snow as my little sister, Nonie, and I started off to our grandparents' house. We were to sleep there overnight. Our parents had given us some tobacco to take to them. We were very excited because snow meant that ni mishomis and nokomis would tell us stories of Nanabosho.

Ni Mishomis tells us these particular kinds of stories in the winter when most of the animals are asleep. Ni mishomis says if the animals heard us telling these stories in the summer, they would come so close to listen that we might find them in our beds!

Ni mishomis and nokomis tell us beautiful stories about how Nanabosho helps our people and how things came to be what they are. Sometimes, they are funny stories about Nanabosho tricking people and animals, or even of his being tricked himself. There are some stories where Nanabosho acts as silly as Nonie and I sometimes do.

When we got there, Nonie wanted to give our gift of tobacco to grandpa, but I made her hang up our coats, instead.

"Ni mishomis, could you tell us about Nanabosho?" I asked, placing the tobacco on the table.

"Mikwech, Nonie and Billy. First we will eat, then we will have a story," he said, taking the tobacco.

After supper, when the dishes were done, nokomis sent us out to bring in some firewood for the stove, and then ni mishomis said, "As soon as the floor is swept, I can start."

Nonie and I quickly swept the floor and, finally, we sat with ni mishomis. He then began his story.

"I will tell you about Nanabosho, our great teacher, and how the Great Mystery first sent him to earth."

Long ago, isan, when the world was new, it is said there was a woman who lived with her husband among the stars, until one day, she alone came to earth.
We know her as Nokomis.

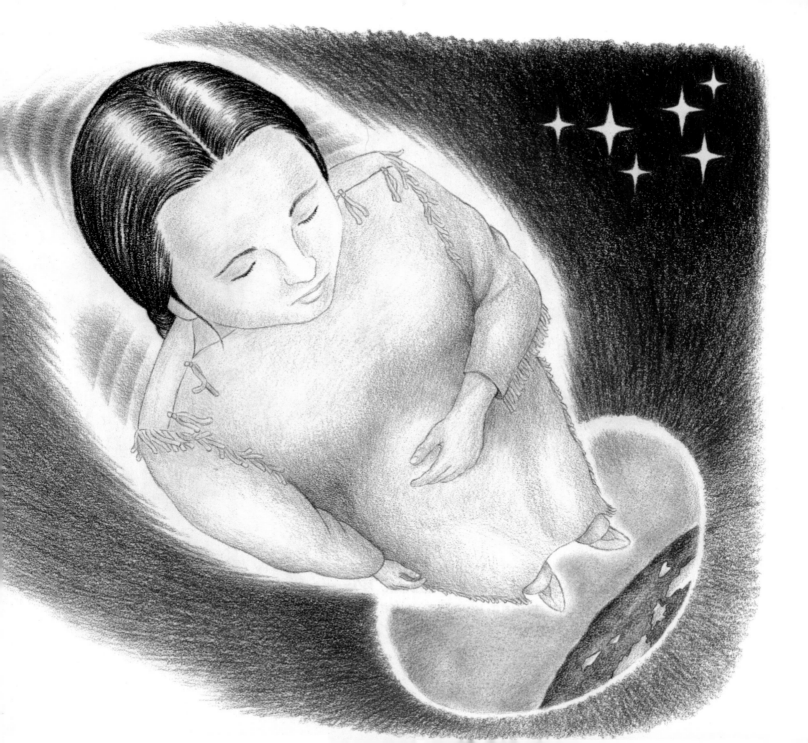

Shortly after coming to this earth, she gave birth to a baby girl whom we'll call Winona. Winona grew to be a very beautiful young woman, wise in the ways of the land and respectful toward her mother.

Every day they would sit by the fire and work. Nokomis
would often tell her daughter, "Ni tanis, I have a great fear of
West Wind."

Nokomis had heard from animals that West Wind was looking for a
new wife. She knew that this wind could be harsh and rough, and she
was afraid that he would take Winona if he ever saw her lovely face.

"Never sit facing west. It could be very dangerous if he saw you facing that direction."

One day, as young people sometimes do, Winona forgot Nokomis's warning. She was so wrapped up in her work on a new pair of moccasins that she sat by the fire facing west.

Suddenly, she felt a cold gust of wind prickle her skin as West Wind happened by. He saw how beautiful Winona was and wanted her for his own.

He blew up a big storm and swept her away with him to the mountains far to the west of her home.

There she had to marry him and keep his house.
Poor Winona was very lonely. She was afraid of West Wind
and his rough, angry ways. Every day she hoped to return to
Nokomis and her beautiful land by the lake.

Nokomis searched everywhere for Winona, until one day, an eagle felt sorry for her and said, "Nokomis, your daughter has been taken by the West Wind and carried far away to the mountains where he lives."

"It is no use then," said Nokomis. "I cannot match his power." With that, Nokomis sadly returned to her home.

One evening as Nokomis sat by her fire, she thought she was being called, but in a whisper,
  "Nokomis, Nokomis, Ni tetam."

At first, she thought it was only a bird calling the distance or a trick of the wind. But when she looked to the west, she saw Winona coming slowly toward her. She ran and took her daughter in her arms.

  "Ni tanis, I have missed you so much," Nokomis said. "I am so glad to see you."

  "Ni tetam, all this time I have been away, I thought of you and our beautiful land. I am with child and I have come home to have my child here, away from his father who scares me so. Ni tetam, I am so tired, I must lie down."

Nokomis led her to the lake and helped her lie down
comfortably. Later that night, Winona gave birth to her sons.
She was so exhausted from the journey that this effort was too
great and she passed on to the land of the spirits. One of the
baby boys was healthy and cried loudly . . .

*. . . while another was weak and
died shortly afterwards.*

"Oh," said Nonie, "this story is so sad."

"In life," ni mishomis replied, "many things are sad. Often out of our sadness, though, can come great strength and great joy."

"How?" I asked.

"Well, we'll see," said ni mishomis.

Nokomis was so sad at the death of her daughter and her
grandson that she couldn't think straight. She took the baby and
wrapped him in moss and soft grass and placed a wooden bowl
over him to keep the animals away.

Then she went off into the woods where she grieved for four days before buying the bodies of her daughter and grandson.

Later that day, while Nokomis was washing away her grief, she suddenly thought, "Oh no! I have forgotten the baby I wrapped and covered! He may have starved to death already!"

Quickly, she ran back to her camp, where she had left the baby. When she found the bowl, she overturned it.

"I have grieved too much," Nokomis cried, "and now something has happened to this baby!"

As she sat, full of new sorrow, she noticed a small white rabbit eating grass. She picked it up and began to pet it.

"Nokomis," said the rabbit, to her great surprise, "do you not know me? I am your grandson, Nanabosho."

With that, the little rabbit changed into her baby grandson.

Nokomis knew then that her grandson was a powerful
spirit who had changed himself into a rabbit because he
had become so hungry.

When the birds and the animals heard his name,
they traveled the earth, telling every living thing that
a great spirit named Nanabosho . . .

. . . *now walks the earth. And very rapidly, the son of West Wind and grandson of Nokomis grew and learned of the world around him.*

From that day on, Nanabosho, who could change himself into anything imaginable, became a great teacher of the Anishinabe in their beautiful homeland.

"This is why," said ni mishomis, "we always say 'bosho' when we greet each other – to remind ourselves of the teachings of Nanabosho. And this is why you must treat everyone and everything with respect. You never know when Nanabosho has changed himself into something around you, and you certainly don't want to be disrespectful to him or anything in Creation."

Nokomis looked at us and took Nonie's hand, saying, "Come, my girl, it's bedtime. There are many more stories to tell, but first, you must sleep on this one. Tomorrow, we will be going out to check our snares. And we will find out more about Nanabosho then."

Other Titles in the Nanabosho Series from Joe McLellan

The Birth of Nanabosho
Nanabosho and the Woodpecker
Nanabosho and the Cranberries (Written by Joe McLellan and Matrine McLellan)
Nanabosho Grants a Wish (Written by Joe McLellan and Matrine McLellan)
Nanabosho Dances
Nanabosho – How the Turtle Got its Shell
Nanabosho and Kitchie Odjig (Written by Joe McLellan and Matrine McLellan)
Nanabosho, Soaring Eagle and the Great Sturgeon
Nanabosho and Porcupine (Written by Joe McLellan and Matrine McLellan)

Other Pemmican Titles by Joe McLellan and Matrine McLellan

Goose Girl